Clown's

Written by Jill Eggleton
Illustrated by Totaea Rendell

Rigby

Clown put on his sock.

"A hole!" said Clown.

Clown put on his pants.

"A hole!" said Clown.

Clown put on his shirt.

"A hole!" said Clown.

Clown put on his coat.

"A hole!" said Clown.

Clown put on his shoe.

"A hole!" said Clown.

Clown put on his hat.

"A mouse!" said Clown.

Labels

hat

coat

shirt

pants

sock

shoe

Guide Notes

Title: Clown's Clothes
Stage: Emergent – Magenta

Genre: Fiction
Approach: Guided Reading
Processes: Thinking Critically, Exploring Language, Processing Information
Written and Visual Focus: Labels, Panels
Word Count: 54

READING THE TEXT

Tell the children that the story is about a clown who is putting on his clothes and he finds holes in everything.
Talk to them about what is on the front cover. Read the title and the author / illustrator.
"Walk" through the book, focusing on the illustrations and talking to the children about the different clothes the clown tries on.
Before looking at pages 12 - 13, ask the children to make a predicition.
Read the text together.

THINKING CRITICALLY
(sample questions)
*   Why do you think the mouse was in Clown's hat?
*   What do you think Clown will do with the clothes that have holes?

EXPLORING LANGUAGE
(ideas for selection)

Terminology
Title, cover, author, illustrator, illustrations

Vocabulary
Interest words: clown, sock, hole, pants, shirt, coat, shoe, hat, mouse
High-frequency words: put, on, his, a, said